I, Too, Am America

LANGSTON HUGHES

Illustrated by
BRYAN COLLIER

SIMON & SCHUSTER BOOKS FOR YOUNG READERS

New York   London   Toronto   Sydney   New Delhi

SIMON & SCHUSTER BOOKS FOR YOUNG READERS
An imprint of Simon & Schuster Children's Publishing Division
1230 Avenue of the Americas, New York, New York 10020
Originally published as "I, Too"
Text copyright © 1925 by Langston Hughes, copyright renewed 1953 by Langston Hughes
Reprinted from: *The Collected Poems of Langston Hughes*, Arnold Rampersad, editor. Copyright © 1994 by
The Estate of Langston Hughes. Published by arrangement with
Alfred A. Knopf, a division of Random House, Inc.
Illustrations copyright © 2012 by Bryan Collier
SIMON & SCHUSTER BOOKS FOR YOUNG READERS is a trademark of Simon & Schuster, Inc.
For information about special discounts for bulk purchases, please contact
Simon & Schuster Special Sales at 1-866-506-1949 or business@simonandschuster.com.
The Simon & Schuster Speakers Bureau can bring authors to your live event.
For more information or to book an event, contact the Simon & Schuster Speakers Bureau
at 1-866-248-3049 or visit our website at www.simonspeakers.com.
Book design by Laurent Linn
The text for this book is set in ITC Berkeley Oldstyle Std.
The illustrations for this book are rendered in mixed media.
Manufactured in China
0312 SCP
2 4 6 8 10 9 7 5 3 1
Library of Congress Cataloging-in-Publication Data
Hughes, Langston, 1902-1967
I, too, am America / Langston Hughes ; illustrated by Bryan Collier.
— 1st ed.
p. cm.
"Reprinted from: The collected poems of Langston Hughes. Copyright
1994 by The Estate of Langston Hughes"—Copyright p.
ISBN 978-1-4424-2008-3 (hardcover)
I. Collier, Bryan, ill. II. Title.
PS3515.U27413 2012
811'.52—dc22
2011002879

I fully acknowledge and appreciate the long hours, timeless dedication, and amazing dignity of the Pullman porters, African-American men who worked as caretakers to wealthy white passengers aboard luxury trains. This practice began after legal slavery ended and lasted until the 1960s on trains that criss-crossed the United States. One day I plan to do a complete study in picture book form that focuses solely on the life and history of the Pullman porter.

—B. C.

I, too, sing America.

I am the darker brother.

They send me to eat in the kitchen
When company comes,

But I laugh,
And eat well,

And grow strong.

Tomorrow,

I'll be at the table

When company comes.

Nobody'll dare
Say to me,
"Eat in the kitchen,"
Then.

They'll see how beautiful I am

And be ashamed—

I, too, am America.

This wonderful and well-known poem by Langston Hughes may be spare with words, but it is loaded with power. It speaks of the relentless courage and dignity the Pullman porters were able to show while working, day in and day out, in a job and in a country where they suffered injustice and unfair treatment and working conditions based on nothing but the color of their skin.

Although Hughes never specified any certain person in his poem, I've created a visual story line that shows how the Pullman porters lived out the message of the poem. My story depicts the true actions of Pullman porters gathering newspapers, magazines, blues and jazz albums, and other items left behind by traveling passengers and then, from the back of the last train car, tossing this bundle into the air, acting as a conduit of culture, a distributor of knowledge to those who couldn't afford these items on their own. In my version of these events, the items lyrically soar through space and time as some land in a cotton field down South in a distant past, discovered by a joyous young girl who will learn from them. And part of this bundle lands in a different, more modern time in a northern cityscape, reminiscent of Langston Hughes's own hometown of Harlem, New York, where there are still eager hands and minds ready to absorb whatever knowledge they can.

I also want to direct your eye to the stars-and-stripes American flag motif, a more subtle way I have tried to convey the message that I took from Langston Hughes's words. It first appears as a light veil over the face of a Pullman porter, but toward the end of the book, during a more contemporary time, it completely covers a mother and son riding the subway. Even later, in the last image of the book, that same boy creates an opening through the flag and peers through it to an unknown future. It acts as a metaphor for the growth of our people in this country, almost invisible during the Pullman porter's time—just as he was even though he worked every day in plain sight—but bolder and stronger toward the end, no longer invisible and ignored. To me, this represents how far African-Americans have come in this country since the Pullman porters' time, and even since Hughes's time, and how bright our future can be.